A Picnic Surprise

Written by Leslie McGuire
Illustrated by Art and Kim Ellis

A GOLDEN BOOK • NEW YORK

Western Publishing Company, Inc., Racine, Wisconsin 53404

"Barbie, what are we bringing to eat on the picnic?"
Skipper asked as she and Ken walked into the kitchen.

"Chicken, potato salad, brownies, and lemonade,"
Barbie answered. "I made everything myself."

"Looks great," said Ken, lifting the cloth that covered
the basket. "Smells great, too. Can I have a quick taste?"

"Your quick taste would be the entire chicken," said Barbie, laughing. "The point of a picnic is to eat the food when you get there, not before you leave!"

"I'm glad we have our bathing suits on underneath our clothes," said Skipper. "We can go swimming at the lake right away."

"I even brought my lucky fishing pole," said Ken.

Barbie, Ken, and Skipper put everything into the car, and off they went. There wasn't a cloud in the sky.

"What a perfect day for a picnic," said Barbie as they drove up into the mountains.

"Oh, look," said Skipper when they got to the picnic area. "There are two deer!"

Sure enough, standing by the edge of the woods was a beautiful doe and her baby.

"I bet they want to eat our picnic lunch," said Ken.

"Don't be silly," said Barbie. "Deer don't like chicken and potato salad!"

"That's because they've never had any of *your* chicken and potato salad," said Ken as he unloaded the car.

Ken found a great spot to put down their picnic basket. It was under a tree, right next to the lake.

"Let's go swimming," said Skipper.

"Let's go out in one of those boats," said Barbie.

"Let's do both," said Ken.

The three of them climbed into a rowboat and rowed out to the middle of the lake.

"Hey, look," said Skipper. "There's a float!"

"I have an idea," said Barbie. "Ken, why don't you row us over to the float. I'll teach Skipper how to dive."

"I'd love that!" said Skipper, jumping out of her seat. The rowboat almost tipped over.

"Whoa!" said Ken. "Don't start diving yet!"

"Ken, you can do a little fishing while Skipper practices," said Barbie.

After Barbie and Skipper climbed onto the float, Ken rowed back to the middle of the lake.

"Here's what you do," said Barbie. "Stand with your feet together and your toes on the edge of the float."

Skipper did exactly what Barbie said.

"Now bend at the waist," Barbie went on, "and point your hands down at the water. Then fall in!"

Skipper broke the water with a big SPLASH!
"Almost perfect," said Barbie. "Now try again."
After Skipper had been practicing for a while, Ken
rowed back over to the float.

"Look what I caught!" said Ken.

Barbie and Skipper burst out laughing when Ken pulled an old boot from the bottom of the rowboat.

"Is that what you catch when you use your lucky fishing pole?" Skipper asked. "We should cook it up for supper!"

"That would taste terrible," Ken said as he made a face. "But speaking of supper, I'm starved. Let's go back to shore and eat."

But when they got back to shore, something terrible had happened. The picnic basket was lying on its side. The napkins were blowing away in the breeze. The potato salad was all over the blanket, and a pile of crumbs was the only trace left of the brownies.

"Oh, no!" said Skipper. "Our picnic is ruined!"

"What a mess," said Ken.

"Look!" shouted Barbie. "That's who wrecked our picnic!"

Ken and Skipper looked. There at the edge of the woods was a little dog with their chicken in its mouth.

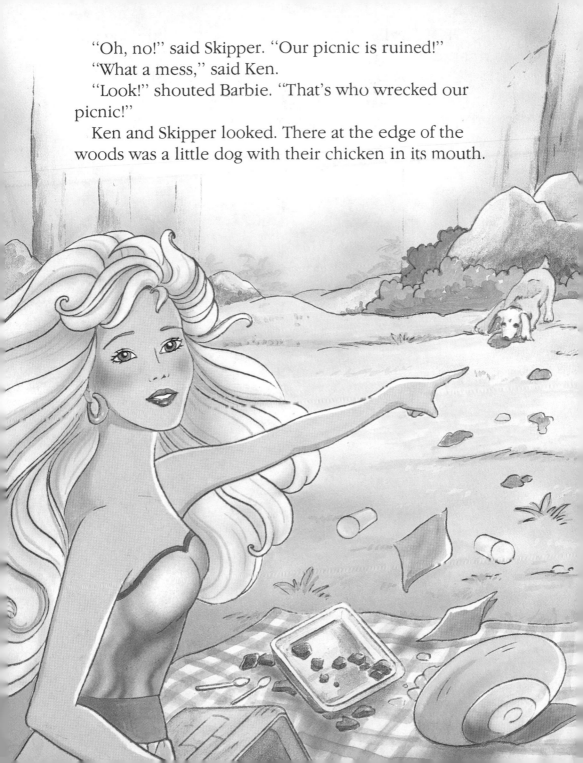

"STOP!" yelled Ken. But, of course, the little dog took right off into the woods.

"Come back with our chicken!" shouted Skipper.

The three of them ran after the dog. They chased it around bushes, over fallen trees, and across a little stream.

Just when Barbie thought she was close enough to
grab the little dog, it disappeared into a hollow log.

"Why bother," Ken panted as he caught up with her.
"We can't eat the chicken now anyway."

"Yuck!" said Skipper.

But Barbie wasn't thinking about the ruined picnic anymore. She was looking inside the log for another reason.

"This isn't just any dog," said Barbie. "This is a mother dog—and she has puppies!"

Sure enough, inside the log were four of the cutest puppies they'd ever seen. The mother dog crawled out and gave Barbie's hand a lick.

"Oooh," said Skipper. "These puppies are so-o-o cute! Can we take them home?"

"I don't think so," said Barbie.

"Why not?" asked Skipper. "I'd take care of them, and I know we could give them a really good home."

"I think they already have a home," said Barbie. "See, here's a tag. This dog's name is Princess, and I bet her owner is very worried about her."

Ken went back to the blanket and got the empty picnic basket. They put all of the puppies in the basket and then headed back to the car. When they drove by a phone booth, Barbie stopped and called the number that was on Princess's tag.

The dog's owner, Mrs. Wells, told them how to find her house, and then said, "Thank you! I'm so glad you found her.

"Thank goodness you're all right, Princess," Mrs. Wells said when Barbie handed the dog to her. "You've been gone for three whole weeks. I've been so worried about you."

Then she turned to Barbie, Ken, and Skipper. "Princess is a show dog, and she doesn't like anyone to make a fuss over her puppies. This is the third time she's run off to have puppies in the woods!"

After a bath, Princess looked a lot more like a show dog than she had that morning. While Skipper played with the puppies, Mrs. Wells prepared a delicious lunch to make up for the picnic Princess had taken.

In fact, she fed them cold chicken, potato salad, brownies, and lemonade!

When they got in the car, Mrs. Wells said, "As a reward for finding Princess, you may have one of her puppies. Come and pick one out in a few weeks when they are a little older."

"Oh, thank you!" Barbie, Skipper, and Ken said together.

"You see," said Barbie as they drove home, "our picnic didn't turn out the way we'd planned. It turned out even better!"